MW01143894

Every Dog

STARRABECK

for Catherine Ireland

1

Before the snow went the work started. Robert had begun winter sports in the field next door, but finished sledging there when the snow became sticky, and tried walking with skis. He got nowhere, became fed up, and gave up. The last snow clouds came in the afternoon and covered all his marks with fresh white. The clouds drifted away, and a daylight moon sat on a hillside and looked about. The moon never quite understands what it is seeing, up so early.

"It was really stupid to try at all," Robert told Mum, when he came in wet through and shivering. "But I won't be able to do it next winter, will I?"

"Not there," said Mum. "We can still see it

1

but it isn't ours any more."

They had sold the field. Something was to be built there. Men had walked about on it during the winter, looking at plans and getting them wet in the rain or frozen in the frost. Then they had gone away, and that was that so far. They had left one pole, put carefully near the middle of the field.

Robert went upstairs and took off his soggy tracksuit bottoms. Downstairs Mum was saying, "You can put them in the washer yourself, you know how."

Robert was saying, "Yeah, yeah, yeah," so that Mum would understand it wasn't man's work to do that sort of thing, even if he did it this time just for once.

And he was thinking of something else. He stood with one leg in the cold bedroom and the other in cold tracksuit, and looked from his window.

Work was starting in the field. Building was going to happen. Men trudged across the snow. Two of them measured with a tape.

The sun came out from the last cloud for a moment, and drew a sharp dark shadow on the whiteness.

There was more measuring. A man with a mallet drove short pegs into the ground, with a thump and a thump, and sometimes a third. The pegs went to make a square, for the corners of the new building, and in a lot of other places too. The final shape seemed like a scribble in the snow, no matter how Robert's eye joined up the dots.

If you're just going to put them every-where, he thought, why measure everything?

Though playing with the tape must be fun.

The last peg went in, thump, thump. The tape was wound up into its reel, the mallet went into the back of a van, the three men into the front, and the van went busily away, its lights flashing and shining.

Mum came up to look from the window too. "It looks small," she said. "Like a kitchen, not like a school." The new building would be the new primary school, complete with indoor toilets, three classrooms, an assembly hall, a kitchen and a library.

"Yeah," said Robert, kicking off the last tracksuit leg – under the bed out of sight.

"I don't understand the shape," said Mum, talking about the new school, and, "Don't just throw them under there," talking about the tracksuit bottoms.

4

Dad came in, then went out again to look over the garden wall, because the big moon was sailing high now, and outdoors was like a thin sort of cold day.

"The layout always seems small at first," Dad said. "Like they've drawn it the exact same size as the plans on the paper."

"They won't fit it all in," said Robert, leaning on the garden wall beside him and agreeing. Anyone could tell that a school wouldn't fit in the tiny space marked out. "I wish they'd had all those rooms when I went to the old school. They have all that at the secondary school."

"I just went to the one here, the same as you," said Dad. "There wasn't a secondary school then, but what we had was big enough for what we wanted to know. But when this is finished it will be the right size for all the stuff kids have to know now."

Robert tried to imagine what it would look like when it was complete and full of kids. But he could not even think what it would be like the next day. He could only think of it now, and suddenly built all the way, he told Dad, not the bits between.

"And we shan't remember what the empty field was like," said Dad. "Unless we try."

I shall only remember the moonlight, Robert thought.

When they went in Mum was thinking of now. She said, "Get that track-suit into the washer, Robert, eh?"

"Yeah," said Robert. But he managed to do it, stuffing both its legs into the black moon of the washing machine's mouth.

"Long rinse," said Mum. "That's all they need."

"I'll tell Oggin, our cat," Robert said secretly, not giving in to household stuff.

Some time in the night the house was still and quiet. There was no TV downstairs, no noise on the road outside, only Dad having a little snore.

Robert woke up because one foot had gone walking on its own and had to wake him because it was too stupid to come in by itself. When it did get back under the covers it walked all over his other foot, and woke that up too.

"You want a long rinse," Robert told it. But he had to wake up to say so. When his eyes opened it seemed like morning light all over the room. But it was moonlight, cold, and not useful, the colours all dim.

There was a noise outside, like an owl, but not quite so. It wasn't Oggin, asleep on a chair.

Robert sat up, made a tent round him-self, warm in the cold bedroom, and looked through the window at the sleeping world.

It seemed not to be sleeping. There was the field, just as he had last seen it, the tops of the pegs like dots, their little moon-shadows on the snow.

There was something else too.

The men have come back, Robert thought, seeing something move in the field, among the pegs.

Someone has put a pony in, he thought next. Are they going to have a school pony? We didn't even have a hamster. And it's not old fat Oggin.

It was not a pony. It was not big enough. It seemed to be eating grass. Perhaps it was a donkey? But it was not a donkey, or a goat, or a sheep.

Lion? thought Robert. He drew the tent closer round him. Perhaps it was time to go to sleep again, with his mind thinking wild thoughts.

Then he knew what it was out there. But the creature lifted its head and looked up at the moon, and it was surely a dog. But dogs do not eat grass like that. Then it opened its mouth and sang out a howl to the moon, and went back to what it was doing.

It was a tall dog, grey in the moonlight, very thin with long legs. It had short but flopped ears, a furry and narrow face with a long muzzle, and a long tail. But was it eating?

9

What was in its mouth? What was it doing?

Very methodically, going from one to the next, all the way round the site, back and forth, betwixt and between, the dog was putting his mouth round a peg, giving it a sharp twist, pulling up each one marking the new building, carrying all away one by one, laying each in a different place, and burying it more or less upright. When each hole was full it sniffed to see that everything was tidy, and went back for another peg. It seemed not to miss any: each one had to be moved carefully to another location.

At last it seemed to have moved them all. It did a last search, sniffed about the tall pole that had gone into the ground first, decided not to pull it out, stood on three legs and wee'd on it, scratched the ground with all four feet, looked at the moon, howled a last howl, and left the field by the gate.

In the next room Dad snored like a crocodile, and Mum did her pretty breathing like bells ringing. Robert collapsed his tent and fell asleep.

Somewhere a rangy dog was looking for its bed. Oggin got off his chair, went downstairs, flipped through the flap, and went out to see about things.

And the moon went on watching.

2

It went on being school for a week or two. Robert forgot about waking in the night. Oggin often went out and came back with cold feet and wet fur to get a warm-up on Robert's face, Oggin 'ogging the pillow, the same as he hogged the hearthrug if he got there first. Robert did not look out of the window.

In fact, with darkness lasting until bus time, and rain lasting all night, Robert did not think at all about the new school marked out with pegs, until one day it was holidays, and sunny, and he got up late and was eating those square cereals two at a time.

There was a machine out in the road, yellow with giant digging legs hitched up, a chimney with a rattly cap on it, and a man getting out of the cab.

He looked round. He leaned on a gate. He scratched his head. The machine chuntered away to itself behind him.

The man looked at a map. He looked at a plan. He tried his mobile phone. Robert watched him find it didn't work up here, even when it was shaken.

"Lost," said Mum. "Turned up in the wrong place to dig ditches for a farmer somewhere else."

Robert was busy using his arm as an excavator to get as many bits of square cereal into his mouth as possible. There was milk everywhere.

The doorbell rang. Mum went to see who it was. Robert managed to get cereal across the room and into the hearth.

The man at the door was the driver of the machine, looking for the site of the new school. He was Oz, from up the village, and Mum knew him and his wife.

"Marked on the map," he said. "The site."

"Right," said Mum, looking at the map. "No problem."

"Just over there," said Robert. "I'll open the gate."

"Digging out the foundations," said Oz. "I'm meant to be. But."

'But' was because the place he had to dig was not marked out as it should be, according to Oz's plan.

"Pegs," said Oz. "Marked out with pegs."

"Saw them doing it, Oz," said Mum. "Yonks ago."

"I know," said Oz. "But they've changed

it, or summat. Got to have the right layout for the walls, or I don't know where to dig."

"I'll show you where," said Robert. "Sort of."

Oz looked at him. Mum looked at him. Robert remembered waking one night, and thought, I could explain, but I'd better not. They won't believe it. I don't believe it. Dogs don't do plans and stuff.

"Yeah," he said.

They weren't believing him even before he said it. He couldn't say it, he could not say, "A dog moved them all." It was impossible to get things right.

Of course he did not even believe it himself. It must all have been a dream. There was no grey thin dog, no little howl at the moon, no pulling up of pegs, no midnight wee against the tallest pole.

There was no dog in his mind, he decided.

"Just saw they'd been changed," he said.

Mum looked at him. Oz looked at him.

"My mobile's out of touch," said Oz. "I'll just walk down to the box . . ."

"Use ours," said Mum.

"Yeah," said Robert.

•

Later on Oz left. The site would have to be laid out again, he said, or all the foundations would be in the wrong place and the blackboards would fall on the kids' heads. The machine clattered its chimney lid, turned in the gateway of the school field, and went away.

"Well?" said Mum.

"No," said Robert. "I didn't do anything, and if I tell you what it was you won't believe me even more."

"Don't you mean even less?" said Mum.

"Yeah," said Robert. "Both."

"Try me," said Mum.

Robert tried her. He told her what he had seen, how the dog had walked about, pulled out the pegs one by one and put them in other places, then gone away after its quick wee.

"Oh well," said Mum, "You think a dog was redesigning the school? It was a dream, that's all. Maybe a dog, or our cat Oggin, maybe you needed the loo. But it was a dream."

"Yeah," said Robert.

"Now you don't believe *me*," said Mum.

A few minutes later no one was quite sure. Robert took her out of the front gate, along the road and into the field, and showed her how the dog had reburied the pegs. Some of them had fallen over, having been buried in snow that had melted.

They were made of wood, about forty centimetres long, and painted white. The tops were hammered down by the mallet, so the edges were bent over and the sides split a little. The pointed ends had mud and scratches on them, for more than half their length.

"You couldn't have pulled these up with your bare hands," Mum said. "I saw them hammered in. You'd need a tool. But I don't know what."

She looked at several more pegs, chose two, and said it was time to go back. She took the pegs with her.

"It's stealing," said Robert.

"They want washing," said Mum. "Then

I'll explain. Well, I won't quite be able to explain . . . but let's see, shall we?"

She rinsed the pegs at the sink, then dried them carefully. Lost it, Robert thought. It's proved.

"Tell me again," Mum said, looking at the pegs. "About your dream."

But Robert could not say any more. He looked at the two pegs, like the horrible teeth of some avenging monster out to get him, and thought quickly that he had promised to go and play football at the other end of the village.

•

After tea Dad said, "Have you finished? Open your mouth."

"You're not going to give me a worm pill," said Robert. "I'm not Oggin our cat." Last time Oggin had that dose he bit several people and severely frightened a chair.

"Well, I don't even need to look," said Dad. "I've seen these pegs, and I believe you. I don't believe you had a dream about that dog."

"Nor do I," said Mum.

"Yeah," said Robert. "Suddenly I saw it in reality and that makes it all right?"

"Well," said Dad, "they aren't your toothmarks on these pegs. You haven't got fangs like that."

Robert had not thought about it, but Mum had. She had seen what was there, not losing her mind totally.

"Dog tooth," said Dad, holding out a peg, indicating the marks where teeth had held, held and pulled. "He got hold with his mouth, shook his head, and got the peg out. Like always, it takes one of the world's great detectives to solve the mystery."

"Me, for instance," said Mum.

"I suppose," said Dad. "Yes, you did see it first, but I would have done if I'd been there."

"But a dog wouldn't have done it," said Robert.

"Those were pulled out by a dog, and you saw him do it," said Dad. "Right?"

"Yeah," said Robert. It was one thing to see it happen, but quite another to have it proved. You don't always want to be certain of something weird. It sometimes feels better not to have the whole truth in your mind. It was impossible for the dog to have done it, and hyper-impossible for it to be true. So now who was losing it?

"It's what Mum said, a dream," said Robert. A dream would be better than the far-

21

fetched truth. "But don't tell anyone. In fact," he went on, giving orders to his parents, "it never happened. Understand."

But the dog didn't know that that rule had started.

3

Building happened slowly. It went downwards at first, with Oz's yellow machine marching in one morning when Robert was racing off for the school bus. It reached most of its downwardness that day, and when Robert got back Oz and the machine had gone, leaving a battlefield with trenches behind them.

"Oh, I didn't watch," said Mum. "I kept wanting to get out there and tidy it all up again." If you once owned a neat field you like to keep it neat.

"We could just go and look," said Robert.

"No," said Mum. "Stay away. The builders used the layout you designed in your dream. They thought it was better, without being pleased with you."

"But we proved it was the dog," said Robert.

"What dog?" said Mum.   "That's the problem, whether it existed or not."

The building climbed out of the trenches back to ground level. It still seemed small for a school. Perhaps the dog thought it was going to be a cramped kennel. But, of course, what dog?

"Best stay out of it," said Dad. "Architect."

"Yeah," said Robert, meaning that he did not agree and wasn't the architect.

Walls began to rise above ground. There were places for doors. The space inside the walls seemed to be filled with other walls. The rooms were going to be cages, Mum said.

"We'll have a look one night," said Dad; but the night was a long time coming.

On school days Robert did not see building happening, and there was no work at the weekends. So walls went up when he was not looking, until half term. But by then the nearest wall was too high to see over, and had only one window to see through, so Robert was no better off.

One evening he thought he saw Oggin climbing about the works, glimpsing him once or twice through that one window. Then he was at the end of the building, looking round from high up. Almost at once he was at the other end. And talking. Saying words like 'Daddy', and 'Look', and being tomcat colour.

Which would have made perfect sense, if Oggin hadn't been lying as ginger as biscuits on the rug, taking up four times as much space as anything else the same size. And Oggin hardly ever spoke words. Oggin never said "Daddy" to anyone.

If I'm not allowed, Robert thought, then that guy isn't either. I'd better . . . and he did what he thought, going out of the door, into the road, past a red car standing there, in at the field gate, across the broken grass, broken stone and dropped sand, past the cement mixer, over the leaky hose, through a tunnel of wood, and in at one of the school doors.

And straight into a cellar with a pond at the bottom. He could have walked through it nearly dry if he hadn't been sitting in it.

Someone did not quite laugh; or something did not quite bark; or a piece of wood creaked; or maybe several bones got bent or broken.

"Hello," said a man. A man with a plan in his hand. He looked at the plan. "I think you are sitting in the staff toilet."

Robert got up at once, even with two broken legs, he thought. Cold water trickled down the backs of them. But otherwise they worked. He climbed out of the hole and stood on some building blocks.

"Right down in the drain," said the man. "I'm Chris Arkwright, and I've come to look at the new school, because when it is finished and we have taken all the boys out of the drains I shall be the new Head Teacher. How do you do?"

"I thought I saw our cat," said Robert. "I mean I knew I hadn't, so I had to look. They think . . ." But he could not say any more of what he was thinking, about pegs being moved, and Oggin making speeches, without getting into even more muddle.

"There are some very thoughtful cats," said the man, Mr Arkwright. "What year are you?"

"Seven," said Robert, knocking thirteen. "I'm at the big school."

"My daughter is in the fourth year," said Mr Arkwright, as if Robert might want to know. "Joanne, this is . . . ?"

"Robert," said Robert.

"Robert, this is Joanne."

Joanne had Oggin-coloured hair. Robert had seen it through the window and thought it was sprawly old Oggin even though he was on the hearthrug.

"Sixth year when school opens," said Mr Arkwright. "If it ever does. The staff toilets are about the openest bit at the moment, as you've found."

Robert felt absolutely ashamed, standing

there in wet trousers with a girl staring at him disapprovingly.

She spoke. "What's your dog called?" she asked.

"It's a cat," said Robert. "Called Oggin."

"No," said Joanne. "Your dog. The tall one with sad legs. Don't you ever feed it?"

"No," said Robert. "We haven't got a dog."

"But he came in with you," said Joanne. "And he looked at you. He was worried until you stood up. He had a worry on his face."

"You should see mine," said Robert.

"That's just mud," said Joanne. "And you're a bit of a comedian. But you might know the dog's name."

"I don't know anything about it," said Robert.

Joanne began to look at him thoughtfully, and disapprovingly, like Mum finding about some little problem such as not combing his hair for a week, when it was only two days after all.

As if he wasn't wet enough, Robert felt something warm and cold and wet on his hand. He felt something breathe on that wetness. He looked down, and the dog he had seen once by moonlight pulling up the marker pegs was licking him gently, and sniffing at his hand. Robert pulled his hand away from the unknown creature. He remembered tooth marks on the pegs, and was sure it was the same dog.

"Steady," said Mr Arkwright. He had been looking at the school plan again, but reached out a hand to stop Robert falling down into the staff toilet again.

"We're not meant to be here," said Robert. "Not me or the dog."

"We came because it's half-term," said Joanne. "He's going back to finish at his old school, and Mum and I are staying in the village in our new house."

"Because we've sold our house down there," said Mr Arkwright. "Like you, I'm just living in the staff toilets until the end of term."

"He doesn't mean it," said Joanne. "Now where's your dog gone?"

The dog had turned away and was looking round the new building. Probably working out which cage belongs to it, thought Robert, since the whole building still seemed small, considering that there was a whole field to build it on.

"I'm not in charge," said Robert. "I don't even know its name."

"Really," said Joanne. "You could find out." She picked her way over the building material and came to the dog. She put her hand on its neck, turned its collar, and read its name. "Coco," she said. "That wasn't very difficult."

The dog wagged its tail on hearing its name.

"Easy, in fact," said Joanne, shaking her ginger head slightly and scornfully.

The dog called Coco went away. It went out through a doorway and that was that. Yeah, thought Robert, now I'm a liar and an idiot. Yeah.

"Junior classroom," said Mr Arkwright, looking round. "Sliding doors, no, that can't be right. Must be the library. Or the kitchen."

The dog was forgotten. Robert began to feel not quite so damp. He began to see sense in the layout of the building, where the infant room was, and the store, and where the boiler would be.

The dog called Coco came back, carrying something black, of a very queer shape. He put it down and waited to be thanked. He was pleased with himself.

"Well I never," said Mr Arkwright, picking it up. "That's going back a bit. That's what teachers used to wear long ago, in the old days, a mortar-board."

"It must be for you," said Joanne, stroking the dog. "And you must feed him, Robert."

"I'm going home alone," said Robert.

4

Robert went home alone, he thought, leaving Joanne and her father trying on the old and ridiculous hat. The hat had a hat-shaped piece for a person's head, a stiff square of black cloth perched on it, and a sort of stringy bobble right at the top in the middle of the square.

No one could know what it really was, Robert decided, walking home in totally wet trousers. And it went from his memory at once, because Mum made him do his own washing again, because, she said, those were his school trousers and you shouldn't have been wearing them.

No, Mum, yes Mum. Yeah.

"One tablet," said Mum. "Wool."

"Tablet?" said Robert. "Is it broken again?

34

Open wide, machine, this is your worm pill."

Towards the end of the week Mum did something strange. She had visitors. Of course, plenty of people came to the house, one way and another, and sat in the kitchen and had Nes or good old Yorkshire, or now and then a drop of Giggle, which gave Mum a snappy head the next day.

But these visitors needed something different. They had the front room, made tidy and polished up.

"I should do this more often," Mum said, getting invisible dust off a chair leg that was already perfect, and giving the clock heart-failure by turning it over and wiping its private minutes with a yellow duster.

"I'm out of this," said Robert.

"You are doing the milk and sugar," said

Mum. "We are having afternoon tea for Mrs Arkwright and her little girl. Mr Arkwright will be talking to the builders. He's the new head teacher of the new school."

"I know," said Robert. "He's living in the staff toilets of his old school a long way off."

"He wouldn't like you hear you say that," said Mum. "Have some manners – and I shouldn't need to tell you that."

"He told me," said Robert. "He said it himself."

"Put some coal in the scuttle," said Mum. "We have to have a fire. Then get yourself tidy and make a good impression."

Robert thought the best thing to do was go out and do twenty other good things. But when he thought of them they never seemed quite enough to fight about.

"And get that cat out of the room," said Mum. "I've just vacced that rug; what will they think?"

"What will Oggin think?" said Robert.

They soon found out. Mum was keeping Robert tame by making him read a book, and Robert was arguing that he'd read one before and they were all the same so what was the point, when the doorbell rang.

"Kettle on," said Mum, going to the door and opening it, "and let those sandwiches alone."

Then she was speaking to Mrs Arkwright, smiling and saying hello, and this is Joanne? Squeak, she went a bit, being so polite, then saying, will your dog be all right in the porch?

And Joanne saying, "but we haven't got a dog."

And Oggin coming out of the room where he had been testing a sandwich, dropping the sandwich, getting to twice his already enormous size and thrice as ginger, shouting out terribly rude things, rising off the carpet, and hurling himself out of the door, not touching the ground. You could see his claws flashing, Robert was sure, the air ripping.

Joanne shrieked. Mrs Arkwright said, "Oh my goodness," Mum said, "What? Robert," Robert not quite able to say anything because he was testing a sandwich too (girly sort of paste, he thought).

Oggin went across the garden like a mad rocket losing its orbit, got into reverse before the wall but still continued forward (but now backwards), hissing like something about to blow up. He landed with all four feet on the

38

face of the wall, face to the ground, fell off it, looked round for the enemy, and sat down, bewildered, shedding growls.

He had seen what Mum had seen, a tall dog on his patch, and having to be seen off. Mum thought the porch was right for it. Oggin thought dogs were best in small pieces all over the landscape.

Mum saw him go straight through the dog. Mum was the one who had mentioned dog.

"Does he often have these attacks?" said Joanne. "Are you sure you haven't got a dog?"

"Where did you get him?" asked Mrs Arkwright, looking wonderingly at Oggin. "The Serengeti?"

Oggin sat for a moment or two on the grass, twitching his tail. He sang a little bit. He had seen a dog. He had carved it up. The bits had run away.   They had learnt their lesson.   He got up, walked proudly indoors, and jumped on the stolen sandwich. He made a huge mess of it, on the hearthrug, and went to sleep on the remains.   He had learned to steal sandwiches from the builders, but not that cucumber was bad for him.

In the end the tea party crept out of the front room and went on in the kitchen, which Dad had built with sale items from his work. Robert and Joanne had eaten enough stuff at last, and got into PlayStation games. Mum and Mrs Arkwright closed the door on their noise; but Oggin slept through it.

Mr Arkwright came to the house after he had talked to the builders.   Oggin took a suspicious look for Dog and let him in.

Mr Arkwright brought with him an old

piece of wood. "Piece of an old school desk," he said. "We found it in the new school. It wasn't there when I went into the building. I think that dog of yours brought it, Robert." That was by way of being a joke, Joanne explained when Robert scowled.

"We haven't got a dog," said Mum. "But we've got a cat and a half."

"Strange," said Mr Arkwright. "This is part of the top of a desk, and if you slide back this brass plate the inkwell is still there. The ink has dried up long ago. It's a curiosity from somewhere, but where I don't know, and why it should arrive next door I don't know either."

No one else knew. Mum brewed fresh tea. She was wondering, really, whether to get out the bottle of Giggle mixture, she told Robert, when she came through to put coal on the fire,

"They are so easy to get on with."

Dad came back – a bit early, or the Arkwrights were staying a bit long. He was happy to have a mug of tea, and some Giggle with it for once, he said.

He looked at the piece of wood. He looked well and carefully. He sniffed cautiously at the inkwell.

"It's from before my time," he said. "But I know it well. See here, where some bad lad cut his initials into the wood? Can you read that?"

"B. W.," said everyone. It didn't mean anything until Dad reminded them who they were talking to, Bernard Wilson.

"My desk," said Dad. "Down in the old school. My desk when I got into the top set, before I left and went to work for my living. When I was stalled of sums, and that, I carved my name. That's what that is, a bit of the old school."

Then he found other things about it, and marks on it. It hadn't been out in the rain, he said. "Nor have I, so what about another wet of Giggle, eh? And something's been carrying it about. Look, Julie," (that was Mum) "at these marks."

"That dog," said Mum. "Those tooth marks. The dog that pulled up all the pegs. Those are his teeth."

"Well, that's accounted for, too," said Dad, thinking and remembering as he spoke. "Our old schoolmistress, Mrs Furlong, had a dog like a lurcher, long legs and no body to speak of, can't remember its name, used to come down to school to meet her, end of the day. She liked the dog better than she liked us, I can tell you.

He must have chewed it once."

"But," said Joanne. She had been listening.

"What?" said Mr Arkwright.

"Nothing," said Joanne.   "I might be wrong."

"Yeah," said Robert, because she ought to be, having orbited to 250,375 in Marauder Alert 2500, while Robert had crashed out at 180,326.

5

Dad was thinking that maybe they'd better get him looked at, you can't tell. Robert heard this remark from the kitchen, where he was drying some dishes, and wondered what he had done. There were plenty of ways of not being perfect, so that shouldn't worry Dad.

"Why?" he asked, abandoning the last dish and dumping the cloth on the nearby kitchen floor "What have I done?"

"Nothing much, as usual," said Mum. "Why?"

"Why, why, why," said Dad "Yeah, I see. Not you, we were talking about Oggin having a wild moment.   He might be allergic to something."

"Hard work and exercise," said Mum.

The lazy, large, healthy, large, cat was lying on his back with his large mouth open and his eyes shut.

"Normal," said Robert.

"Out of this world," said Dad. "Meaning, alien."

Robert felt a good turn coming on, now he did not have to be looked at. He went back into the kitchen, picked the cloth up from the floor, and dried that last dish. It still looked clean

Later in the week, or it might have been the next week but Robert was not counting, he met Joanne coming across the village green. He was busy taking no notice, and she did not say hello, or smile, or anything friendly.

"I've been thinking," she said, starting straight up like a friend, no hello. "You know

46

that dog of yours."

"I've seen it," said Robert. "No."

"And your cat," said Joanne.

"It was sick in the night," said Robert.

"I was sick in the night once," said Joanne. "In my Mum's shoes. I got them out from under her bed in the dark. I thought they were the potty."

"Well, see you around," said Robert. "Oggin just did it all down the stairs. Cucumber."

"We'll get to your cat in a moment," said Joanne. "We're talking about that dog. Remember?"

"No," said Robert. "You were talking about it. I wasn't."

"Well, I didn't think I was," said Joanne, even though the last words she had spoken said the opposite quite clearly.

"Yeah," said Robert, hitching up his book satchel and starting to lean towards going home now, at once, thank you, good-bye, even without the words.

"At least," said Joanne, "I wasn't sure. "You know when I came to your house?"

"Did you?" said Robert, forgetting about it at once, having only scored 180,326 in Marauder Alert 2500. "I don't remember, yeah, do I?"

"And your cat was funny," said Joanne.

"A bit of a comedian," said Robert. "My mum will be waiting for me, O.K.?"

"As if he had seen a dog," said Joanne, carrying on through Robert's interruption.

"The one you are talking about," said Robert. "Or you aren't?" Then he thought, I am being nasty to a fourth year, which isn't fair, even if I am allergic to it. "Go on." He stood still and listened, to make things right.

"There wasn't a dog," said Joanne. "At your house, you know."

"Yeah, yeah," said Robert.

"But your Mum thought she saw one."

"She gets like that," said Robert.

"But no one else did."

"Except our Oggin," said Robert

"But if there wasn't one there," said Joanne. "Only your Mum talked about it . . ."

Robert considered the matter for a second or two. He leaned in the direction of home so far that his back leg lifted from the ground and started him walking – not his fault at all – and knew what to say.

"We forgot to explain," he said. "No

mystery at all. My Mum said 'Dog', and of course our cat Oggin understands English without any problems."

"That would account for it," said Joanne. It was not the answer she wanted, but Robert was walking away, and she could not reply.

Only Mum had something to say. "I saw you talking to your little friend." She often liked to recommend girls to him, usually because they had good manners in spite of being completely ugly – as if I care, Robert always thought.

"Did you clear up your cat sick?" he asked. "I can't go upstairs until you do."

When Oggin was awful he belonged to someone else, probably.

•

One Friday wagons came morning and

afternoon to the new school, spinning out grey and scrapy concrete from the churns on their backs. Inside the building men compacted the slurry with vibrating rods, tamped it down level, and left it to harden where it lay.

Late that night they were still in there, by floodlights hung from the roof rafters, smoothing the surface when it was firm enough to walk on but soft enough to make glossy.

Robert saw the evening work begin when he went down to the village hall to play badminton. It was ending when he left, the floodlights were going out and a pick-up truck was having men crowd into it for the first short journey to the pub.

The dog appeared again, limping skinnily across the village green, away from the old school, with an obviously sore front foot.   It was carrying something in its mouth.   It stopped every few paces and gathered the thing together to stop it escaping. It put one front paw on it while it licked the other foot, the sore one.

Robert thought it had a rabbit. This was a rabbiting sort of dog, quick and sharp and poacherish.   But, Robert thought, it was not acting quite sensibly.   A real poacher dog would have killed the rabbit by now and carried it quiet by the neck.

A puppy, Robert thought next. It wouldn't bite that.   Then he remembered the dog standing on three legs and weeing on the post before the new school had been started. So that was a dog, not a bitch.

But what living thing would it carry about?

The dog went slowly up the road ahead of Robert, past Robert's house, and to the new school.

It won't get in, Robert thought. There were wire gates in all the doorways to stop visitors.

"They don't want to be responsible for anyone getting hurt in there," Dad had said.

Later that night Oggin woke with a roar on Robert's bed, and scrabbled at the window. Robert woke too, and looked out with him. Oggin sang.

He was singing at the dog. It was walking away from the school, but not very well. Both forefeet were hurting it now, and it had to stop every few paces and lick then, and then limp on.

"Just go to sleep," said Robert to Oggin.

"O.K.," said Oggin, distinctly, and curled

up again. Robert did not wonder at it. He already knew Oggin spoke English, and went to sleep himself.

Saturday followed, shopping with Mum and rain all day; and Sunday, visiting Grandma at the farm, sorting sheep from lambs with the farm lads, without being noticed. But Monday woke with a jolt, before Robert had got very far out of bed.

There were shouts at the school, like a playground quarrel, then a knocking at the door.

"Have they come for you?" Dad asked. "There's something wrong at the new school."

The men wanted to use the telephone, please, to get to the boss because their mobile was out of range. Someone had got into the school over the weekend and vandalised the new hall floor, digging a hole in it.

And there were bloodstains, probably pools of blood.

And a nasty smell, blimey mate, as if something from long ago had been dug up somewhere else and reburied here – it wasn't like that when we laid the floors.

Dad left for work. "I know it's not you," he said. "You've got a perfect alibi and don't smell like that. Besides, you're not daft. Was it our Oggin smelling? Oggin, they'll be on for you this time."

But Oggin was thinking about breakfast.

6

When Robert got home from school that afternoon he knew something was wrong. Or if not wrong, then slightly miraculous. Someone was up in his room, playing Alert 2500. It must be Oggin, of course, at another stage of his destiny to rule the world.

Oggin being at the same time inside the kitchen window where the birds wouldn't see him, ready to leap through the glass and catch them.

"Joanne," said Mum. "She's been here all day."

"Death to aliens," said Robert. "Come on, Oggin."

Joanne was just crashing out in the upper 190 thousands. She kindly offered Robert a turn at his own machine. It was the reverse of a miracle.

"We didn't have school today," she said. "There was an emergency and we had to go home, so I got dumped here. I didn't mind, Robert."

"So?" said Robert. Not in my room, he thought, but that had already happened and here she was. "What's wrong with school?" Joanne, of course, was talking about the old school, where she went now.

"They didn't know what was in a broken jar," said Joanne. It had fallen from a high shelf during the night, she said, and broken into thousands of pieces. "Of glass, of course," she said, when Robert had a thought about jam. Or lots, anyway. No one knew what was in it, though certainly not jam, because no one had ever taken out the stopper. "And no wonder," Joanne went on, "because there was a horrible smell. So they thought it might be something poisonous, and sent us all home. I came here all day. I wish you'd been here all day too."

"No way," said Robert. And, "Yeah," meaning 'Never, mate'.

Then he had to walk her to her house, but he thought nobody saw him doing that.

"Big green jar," said Joanne. "Huge. A million pieces, so we didn't have to do spelling."

"Big green jar?" said Dad, when he had finished his tea and was going out to play snooker. He had got too firm for badminton, he thought. "I know the one. Fancy still having that in the old school. I'll tell you about it one day."

But no one remembered particularly about it for the time being. It went clearly out of Robert's mind after a few days. He was only hoping vaguely that Joanne didn't have another day off school and get allowed into his computer, or even his room at all.

He was coming back from badminton one evening. He had been working hard, because some people were so small and agile it was difficult to keep ahead, especially when you wanted to ignore her. It was the middle of summer and still light until midnight, and it was nowhere near that time. He saw perfectly clearly what was going on.

The dog was dancing, he thought, on the village green. Its feet were not hurting it. He watched.

He had another thought at the same time,

about what might have hurt the dog's feet so that they bled and had to be licked (by the dog).

Millions of pieces of broken green jar, he thought. Sharp, cutting glass, all over the floor; enough to close a school.

But thoughts are not evidence, even if they want to go together. The only evidence he had now was of the dog dancing.

Sometimes it was a small dance, nearly in one place. Dancing feet, pointing muzzle, ears going up and down, the occasional snappy bark. But what was the dog dancing with, because it could not be making up the different movements? It was now on its elbows, now sitting down, now pushing with its nose at something or nothing. Then it would leap into the air and fly across the grass and whisk round like a sheepdog turning sheep. Then it would hunt and crouch and eye something.

A touch of the Oggins, Robert thought. It's playing with something. Was there anything there? Or was the dog having a mad imagination?

Once it left the green and shot across the road. Oz, in his blue car, put on his brakes and shouted. Mrs Oz, beside him, told Oz off for going fast enough to stop.

The dog flourished its tail, watered Oz's front wheel, went on to the grass again, and rounded up its imaginary charge. That appeared to be still there and occupying the dog's fancy.

There was a change. All at once the dog lost sight, or smell, or whatever, of the thing it was hounding along. The dog sniffed, listened, looked, stood on its hind legs and did all three again.   It sat down on its haunches and sang a little. It lifted its muzzle and howled.

It had another look round on the grass, smelling everything, frowning at tall weeds, listening to birds flying overhead.

Then it had a doggy look at a tree, sorting out who had been there and when, and left a message for other dogs. Dogs don't care who's watching

It nodded to Robert, waved its tail, and walked away.   Robert looked away for a moment, and the dog had got out of sight.

I know cats are like that, Robert thought, or at least one is. But dogs? Can they be un-there when they want? It's a bit strange. And went home.

•

"I don't know whether it was physics, or chemistry, or mechanics," said Dad. He was remembering forty years ago, when he had been at school with a big green glass jar.

"Science," said Mum. "That's what they all are."

"We had a black-and-white television," said Dad. "No science. It was all magic. Nearly all magic. I think this was witchcraft."

Now he had remembered about it he forgot to tell Robert. He was like that: he considered that you knew what he was thinking. They're all like that, Mum often said.

"Yeah?" said Robert, meaning something like, 'We believe you so far, but tell us the rest and we shan't be able to.'

"Nowadays they just have demon– strations," said Dad. "But in my time they had

63

experiments, and the best bits were when they went wrong. They don't like it when demonstrations go wrong. I wish I could remember what this experiment was about, but that's science for you."

Once he had worked out what he was remembering he was all right. The top set had seen the experiment. It was in the days before education got really going and trapped everyone for twenty years, but the teaching lot were visiting schools to show off to the boys how exciting it would be if they let you do it. They didn't do anything for girls, he thought.

"Blanket stitch," said Mum. "Usually."

"And it wasn't bad," said Dad, thinking about it and not remembering to say until Robert made him.

There was this stinking stuff, Dad told him.

Grey lumps the scholars hadn't to touch. Kids in school were called scholars then. But when the visiting teacher wasn't looking he and someone else, probably Oz, had nicked some and dropped it in an inkwell.

"I sniffed it the other day," said Dad. "On that bit of desk the new teacher brought in. It doesn't niff now, but it did that day at school."

He wasn't clear about what happened next. There was a bang, like an explosion. A window-pane got broken and slithered down outside. But that wasn't the green jar bit. That was next, and seemed to involve a whirlwind that scattered paper about, and knocked the blackboard over, and got out of hand. Science, or whatever, was good, Dad had thought. But Oz thought it was too much of a romp for a steady person and went into machinery for a living. Dad had done the wild thing, he said, and worked for B & Q hardware store.

The whirlwind had been put in the green glass jar, the stopper went in like lightning, and wouldn't come out. What was inside was still swirling the next day. "It's done it ever since," said Dad. "And now burst the jar at last, smell and all. Fancy me remembering all that this long after."

7

There was Sports Day, there was the whole end of the summer term crashing out. There was a report. Some people scored 250,375, Robert heard. He had got his usual 180,326. He sort of explained.

"Life isn't a space game," said Mum, seeming disappointed, not thinking at all like that. "'Does not concentrate on these subjects.' Why Robert?"

"They'll manage without him," said Dad.

For a few days it was easy to concentrate on holidays, and then it was hard, because friends were away, the weather was dull, and people tended to want the TV for soaps when Robert needed it for some of the old games.

He watched the building next door for a

time most mornings, but that was dull too. Men were busy all the time, but nothing seemed to change, because it was all drains and wiring going on invisibly inside the high walls.

Once the dog Coco stood in the field all morning watching a hole. Interesting sounds were coming out of it. "Underground water," said Oz, delivering bundles of roof wrapped in plastic sheeting. "That's to drain it off down the hill."

"Rabbits," said Robert, because dogs have sense about such things.

"Maybe," said Oz, and got technical with the tail-lift of the wagon, and told Robert to stay out of the way while he delivered the load.

Then the load sat there for days. Nothing happened anywhere. Even Joanne was not there to be avoided, having gone to Greece for three weeks. She'll just tell me about it when she gets back, Robert thought, seeing her go wearing a classy sort of sun hat and stylish sunglasses.

A day or two later Robert went to Grandma at the farm, where there was plenty to do because the hay was being got, and the cows were to drive in twice a day. It began as a weekend, and became a week, then a fortnight, and then to feel like lasting for ever.

But there was a day when Dad came for him. Robert had to put his trainers in the boot, because they had been following the cows twice a day, and that was only the outsides, Dad said.

At home Oggin ignored him, but was very interested in the trainers, which had not been allowed into the house. Oggin buried them, scrape, scrape, sniff, scrape, scrape, sniff, disgusted look.

"See what I mean," said Dad.

Next door, in the field, the new school had its roof on, up and complete. The next morning there was rain, and it treated the roof as if they both knew what to do, running down it and clattering down the fall-pipes and spluttering into the drains.

There were lights on inside the building, as if people lived there, though they wouldn't do that. As if school had started.

Paths were being made, a simple playground, a gate, a drive and parking places.

A shining school kitchen came in in pieces. There were chairs in stacks, tables in packs, cupboards in racks; there were classroom carpets, going in whole in a roll, coming out as little extra strips and snips. There were vertical blinds to keep the sun out of the windows that were meant to let it in. There was a kitchen fridge that wouldn't go through the door.

"No desks?" said Dad. "Not like my day. You can't carve your initials in little plastic tables, and no one will remember you."

Not only delivery men and van women had been bringing things to the school. The dog called Coco was going in and out too. As usual, each person thought he belonged to someone else, usually Oz.

"I've known a dog like that," said Oz. "But it was a bit since, so it can't be the same one. He just slips in and out like it was all doorways up there."

"Eating the lads' dinners, perhaps," said

Dad.   He and Oz were leaning on Dad's gate looking at nothing and talking about it too (said Mum), waiting for tea.

"Doesn't do that," said Oz. "Just wanders about.   Mind you, we thought he had a sandwich wrapping the other day, but when he dropped it it was nothing but an old exercise book full of sums the kids had done in pencil. Right old. Pounds, shillings, pence."

"Yards, feet, inches," said Dad.

"Worse," said Oz. "Remember rods, poles, and perches, acres, roods, furlongs?"

"Mmn," said Dad.   "Like, not very well. The new metric stuff is easier to remember."

"And bad to work with," said Oz.   "Just numbers, nothing to get hold of."

"So what happened to the book?" said Dad.

"In the skip," said Oz.

Mum said, when she heard about it, that it would be interesting.

"Is that a spare sausage?" said Dad, changing the subject entirely.

So it was Mum who went out to the builder's skip and found the old exercise book full of ancient measurements. "Fancy getting that stuff right," she said, looking at it. "Farthings, remember farthings?"

"I blame Oggin," said Dad, and got a dishcloth thrown at him for vulgarity.

•

The workmen left the site. People came and officially looked at the new school, and then complained about things. Mostly they said it was damp. Dad knew about that. Oz knew about it. Mum dealt with it. She went every morning and opened the windows and doors, and every evening to close them again, to let out the air full of building water.

Robert went with her the first time or two, and found a bright new building too good for kids, he said. It would be better as a college, he decided.

"Now, this wasn't here last night," said Mum, finding a small painted cupboard that didn't match anything else and was sitting in a classroom. "And Mr Arkwright isn't back yet, so who brought it in?"

It was a little hanging cupboard, with a projection upwards at the top with a hole in it for the nail it would hang on. The cupboard's door was slightly open. Inside there were two shelves and an upright compartment. One shelf held some soft thick paper, pink, with unreadable blue writing across it.

Robert thought it should be in the toilets. Pink for girls. But Mum knew better, though she didn't understand what was going on.

"Blotting paper," she said. "A ream of it, hundreds of pieces. A whole page has been blotted, so it comes out in mirror writing."

The other shelf had a school register in it, dating from 117 years ago to 94 years ago, every page carefully filled and signed, and on the cover a label with the name of the old school down on the green, but called an Elementary School, not a Primary School.

In the upright compartment was a tall earthenware bottle, with a dried up cork. The label on that said it was One Quart of Blue-Black Patent Ink.

"Well more than a litre," said Mum,

"judging by bottles of Giggle."

"And it's all been drunk," said Robert, shaking the bottle gently.

"Put the cupboard on the table," said Mum, taking the ink from him because they were standing on the new classroom carpet. She put the ink safely back, but took out the blotting paper. "I'll have a read of it in the staff toilets," she said. "Mirrors there."

"You'll fall in," said Robert, and left her to it. He knew about the staff toilets.

He had another look at the cupboard. There must be obvious signs on it, he was sure. And there were. On the high part at the top was more than a hole for a nail. There were clear marks in the paint, where something had bitten and held – clearly bitten, held, and carried. And a tall dog could carry this small cupboard complete, from old school to new school.

Almost as if it knew what it was doing; as if it had clear ideas about schools. But what could dogs know, or do; and why?

8

During the night Oggin woke Robert by walking on his face with warm feet with slightly prickly edges. And he could buy some new trainers, Robert thought.

Oggin had no message for Robert. Robert's face merely happened to be on his track to the door. He just went out.

Robert rubbed his face, sat up, pulled up the duvet, and listened to the song. Then he knew there should be no song, and it wasn't a song but someone crying a bit. Sort of lost, he thought. He opened the window wider and heard the noise better. Dog, he decided, but it wasn't a dog noise. Or Oggin.

It came from down the field, the new school. The only thing showing there, in the dark shadow against a sky nearly as dark, was a little yellow eye, which was the illuminated doorbell.

There would be no one about there, or the security light would be on. Unless someone, this little kid, too small to set it off, was there. Definitely there, making a sound.

Dad woke when Robert crossed the landing. Mum said, "Be careful," without waking up. Dad got out of bed, listened at Robert's window, pulled overalls on and said he would take a look, so stay here.

But Robert went with him. There was more light out here in the open than in the house. They saw Oggin sitting on the wall, colourless, a shadow among shadows, Oggin taking no notice of the mournful sound coming across the field.

Silently out of the garden gate, silently in at the school gate, click free, no rattle. I would be afraid by myself, Robert thought. But not with Dad. But I can tell what it would be like, I could feel it if I'm not careful.

Then, blap, the security light went on, showing Robert in his pyjamas, Dad in his overalls, and the little crying noise had stopped. Robert had a sudden thought about surveillance cameras, and could they see through clothes?

"Well," said Dad, "we'll go back. I know it's nothing, but I don't understand it."

"What?" said Robert.

"Oh, wait till we get in," said Dad. And when they were in the house again he said what he thought it was, but said he couldn't account for it happening here, and we'll ask

Oz, he remembers it too. Robert went back to bed, closed his window, and wondered.

Oz remembered in the morning. "Yes, Bernard," he said. "Long time ago, but I dare say it went on ever since. The old school was haunted. One of the children haunted it, went off to be a chimney sweep the minute he left, and the first job next day was to come back to the school, climb up inside, and sweep the chimney. And he never came down again. Stayed as a ghost, crying in the chimney. That's what they say, that's what folk heard."

"And now," said Dad, "he's in the new school."

"Where there's only a flue for the oil-fired boiler," said Oz. "Nothing you'd sweep. So what made him shift his place?"

"So, what do you think, Robert?" Dad

asked, maybe wanting to know.

Robert wanted to ask a silly question, on the lines of, Have you examined the sweep for toothmarks? Because whatever carried a little cupboard across, or an old exercise book, could have carried a ghost just as easily. Or, and Robert remembered another thing the dog had done, one evening herding some thing like a live thing from the old school to the new . . . the dog not being big enough to carry any child . . . and Robert decided to forget that, or at any rate not mention it. "Yeah," he said, and left it at that.

But the real reason for saying nothing was different. He suspected that Oz and Dad were teasing him about ghosts and sweeps, and that it had been the night wind along the roof that had haunted him. Or he tried to suspect it, yeah, without deciding anything.

•

The next night there was plain loud noise round the new school. It woke Robert all by itself, without the help of Oggin. He knew what it was. You don't farm all the holiday without knowing that noise. Dad came thumping out of bed, dragging on his overalls and talking to himself.

This time Robert went out to help Dad. There was no ghost about this time, and Dad was saying that it was his own fault, forgot about it, should have said, he wouldn't know I'd sold the field.

This time of year a farmer from a mile or two away always put his sheep in the field, using the top gate. So now the new flowerbeds, the newly rolled out carpet of turf, the fresh drive, the playground, were all being used by forty sheep. Not for parking, or playing, or planting, but for trampling.

And the school opening in three days, already made clean and tidy. Dad and Robert raced round in the dark getting the sheep out. And did a shadowy tall dog help them, over the far side, not very clearly? A dog that knew about school and how it was run?

"I'll sweep clean in the morning," said Dad. "It'll be a hosepipe job on the tarmac."

Robert was too far out of breath to say what he would do. There would be time to tease Dad about it, if it was necessary to sort out about chimney sweeps being lost in school chimneys. Chimney sweep, chimney sheep.

•

Mr Arkwright came back from his holiday just

before the school was to open. Robert spent his time avoiding Joanne, because she was sure to have things to show and tell him forever. All he had to show from his holiday was a pair of trainers, and even those only made a story because Mum had dug the old ones up, and put them in the bottom of the bin.

Mr Arkwright was puzzled one evening about something in the new building, a soft bundle of knotted threads. He brought it to show Mum. She was now the school caretaker, and it might be her cleaning rags. But he had known there was more to it than that.

"There've been things I can't explain, like that painted cupboard," said Mum. "I left that in there. But this I can't understand at all."

Joanne was there, picking at the bundle. "It's not just a tangle," she said. "It's like writing, all joined up, but not on a page, all sorts of words. If you are careful you can hold them in your hand. Some of them are the wrong way round and at first I thought they were Greek letters."

Showing off foreign stuff, thought Robert.

"Every one spelt wrong," said Mr Arkwright, picking at the knots, which were like wire but pliable as cotton. "As if all the mistakes ever made by children had come to the new school to be made again."

As they touched the threads, they fell to dust, 'nesessery' and 'pudal' and 'betuaful' and 'wite' and 'achally' and 'ustiful' and 'trew' and 'Ingland' and 'wishdom' and 'ereplain' and 'hapnec'.

"In my opinion children don't need any help to spell wrong," said Mr Arkwright.

"They do it by instinct. Joanne once couldn't spell 'I', but now it's her best word."

Then he thanked Mum for not being funny about the bundle of words. She went across to the school with him, to throw the dusty bundle into a cupboard as a curiosity, and do more cleaning ready for the opening in a day or two. Robert and Joanne followed, not together, no way, but going in the same direction.

They all went in through the staff door (beside the illuminated bell push). There was a little entrance hall, then the school hall. There were a few scraps of paper on the entrance hall floor, and Joanne picked them up, saying she didn't know she'd dropped them.

They all went through the door to the school hall. The ceiling lights were on, but Mr Arkwright twiddled the switches, because the light was not right. It was not pale, but thick in some way, not quite bright enough for its colour.

Everyone stood still, because there was an odd sensation in the room, as if something had just stopped moving. Then the light brightened, wavered, and swayed. The room was full of swirling paper falling from the ceiling, where it had masked the light. There was a faint horrible smell. Paper spiralled to the floor and settled there, rustling.

9

The other side of the hall sat the dog called Coco, wagging his tail gently, looking pleased. A curl of pink paper fell like a collar round his neck. He got up and went into the infant room.

"Go and fetch your father for the smell," said Mum. "He's the one who'll know."

Mr Arkwright was picking up paper, to see what the writing on it was. There was a neat row of perfect words printed in curved and swirling lettering. Under that row was a copy in ink made by some child. "Long ago," said Mr Arkwright. "This is a copybook: you copied perfect writing until you could do it. Only infants do a bit of that these days, one letter at a time."

Mum was picking paper up. "It's old

rubbish," she said.   "Out of the old school I suppose.   Robert, get your Dad, see if he knows the smell."

Robert ran home.   Joanne ran with him, thinking this was an important occasion on which to be associated with Robert.

"Smell?" said Dad, quite comfortable in an armchair.   "Give it here then."   But he had to get up and come out and experience the smell in the school hall.

"Phwah," he said.   "That's it.   Looks like you had the whirlwind with it too, same as happened when I was a lad.   That time it got the blackboard.   I heard it get out of the jar." But he no longer believed in what he remembered, and thought he had made it up. But the smell was realistic, and he opened the windows to let the night in and sweep it away.

This time, he found, it had pulled down the vertical blinds in a heap on the cupboards. He stayed to hitch them all up again, and when all the old school copybooks and folders of printed sums (all filled in wrong and marked with crosses) and lists of lessons, and time-tables, had been gathered up and put in the bin, everybody went home.

At the door Mr Arkwright turned back. "Your dog's still in here," he said. It wasn't worth correcting him; and in any case there was no dog in the building. So that was that. "Tomorrow night," he said. "The big opening. I hope you can all come."

"I'll open up at seven," said Mum. "And get the benches and chairs out, and set up the platform."

•

The next evening Dad helped with benches, Robert with chairs, and Joanne came to put flowers on the tables. There was to be an opening and welcome and showing off of the new building, and then tea and bits of stuff to eat.

"You bring your own," Mum told Robert. "And don't let that dog in – we'll get the blame if it goes with everything."

People began to turn up soon after seven. Joanne was on one door, her hair brushed out wild and ginger as Oggin. Robert kept the side door. Children from the old school sat on the benches and looked at the food. Governors sat on the platform along with people from the Education Department.

At half past Mr Arkwright came in and shook hands with all the Governors and people like that. Mrs Arkwright followed, and then went to sit with Joanne at the end of the benches.

The lights were dimmed or switched off, and a lot of speech-making began from the platform, people being glad to welcome everybody, a new start, our old school served us well but our needs change; and the same things from another person, but saying 'your old school had served you well'. And then a list of what it cost, including actually (which made Dad look odd) how much had been paid for the site, so that the whole world knew what money he had made.

Robert had left the side door and got near the end of the tables and saw his hand crawling out to save a stray sausage roll from being unhappy on its own.

But he didn't manage to capture it. The door he had just left opened and closed with a thump and a rattle. Everybody looked at him, because it was his door. Mum looked at him most, seeing where his hand lay on the table.

So he was doing two things wrong, he found – the sausage roll and the door. And he hadn't done both of them, or either of them.

There was more rattling by the side door. Mum nodded her head, to mean that Robert should see about it, stop it rattling, let the people in, or out, or something, can't you do anything right?

In the shadows by the side door something rattly was waiting for him. It crunched, but not breakably, under his foot. It jangled against his shin, metallic and glassy. It also had a smell, like something mechanical and old-fashioned, not quite heating oil but less heavy and more bright.

Paraffin, Robert knew.   It was used at Grandma's farm for cleaning machinery and for the shippon lamps, if the electricity failed.

And here was a lamp, at his feet, smelling of its own fuel. It had a glass shade, which had jangled, and the rattle of the lamp was from the chains that hung round it.

Robert saw how to pick it up. And did so. It hung from his hand, all complete and ready to go, the glass shade not very clean, the glass chimney inside that cobwebby, the brass tank brown and grimy, a slight sticky dribble on the handle, as if it had been carried in a mouth . . .

Speeches stopped.   Everybody looked at Robert, except the kids at the front, because he was behind the bigger people behind them.

"Robert?" said Mr Arkwright.

"*Robert!*" said Mum.

"I'll give you a hand," said Dad, stepping through the people. "When did you get this?"

"It just came in," said Robert, handing the whole thing to Dad. "Somebody brought it in."

By now Oz was looking too, and not the only one. He said, "I know that object. That's the old school lamp, from before they had the electric. Do you remember it, Bernard?"

"I do," said Dad, hoisting the lamp high. "Well I never, another forgotten thing come from the old school to the new. Someone's doing this job, in all sorts of ways. Get the long ladder, Oz."

Dad and Oz took over the meeting for a time. Oz went up the ladder to the ceiling and located a hook. Dad handed up the lamp, and Oz hung it.

"You might have given it a wipe," said Mum. "Look at it."

So it came down again, and was made more respectable. Mum did that, and other mums took the opportunity to make the tea and bring the pots in and start filling cups. Things were going to be eaten and drunk, and speeches were judged to be over.

When the lamp was up again, not glittering, said Mum, but not a total disgrace, Oz lit the two wicks (which had been trimmed with new school scissors), adjusted the flames, and put the chimney back over them. He waited for the glass to warm up, then turned the flames up.

Mr Arkwright put out the electric lights.

There was a sort of darkness for a time, until eyes were used to the glow. People began to say how comfortable it was, it just needs a fireplace and a grate and big fire like in the old days, not all this modern smart stuff.

Somebody dropped something. Mum thought it was bound to be Robert, and other parents were sure their child was disgracing itself.

But it was no person. The dog, Coco, was standing by the table. It had walked in carrying a metal basin, and dropped it on the shining new wooden floor.

"It's just like . . ," said Dad.

"It could be the same," said Oz. "But it's so long ago it can't be."

The dog stood by the basin, looking about hopefully. It put its head down and pushed the basin across the floor, and looked up again, expecting something.   It obviously knew the rules.

But did anyone else?

10

"I wouldn't be so daft as to believe it," said Dad. "Would I? Oz, would I? Anyone, would I?"

"But it is very like," said Oz, moving his head up and down. And one or two people in the room, some parents and some grand-parents, made noises and gave their own nods of agreement.

"It wants a sup of milk," said Dad. "Milky tea, I'd say."

"Like in the old days," said Oz. "If it's, well, you know . . ."

"That old basin used to be in the porch," said someone in the third row. "In the old days."

"Dog used to come down at the end of

school," said Oz, "and do just that until Mrs Furlong gave it some milky tea. Coco, they called it, her and Mr Furlong. I mean, it was their dog, not the school's."

"She would have known what to do," said someone else. "She always did it, as often as it came. She liked it better than us."

"And then," said Dad.

"But that won't happen," said Oz, shaking his head this time, not nodding it.

This is daft, Robert was thinking. Am I supposed to have kept it out? It didn't come through the door . . . but how did it get in?

At that moment the door creaked. An old door would rattle. This one was new, but it creaked. Someone, something, was trying to push it open. Someone used to normal doors in ordinary houses. Someone, something, pushing from outside. But school doors these day open outwards, so it's no good pushing.

Just sort of look, thought Robert, just sort of pushing the door open a little.

A ginger foot came round the edge. Now he knew which way to pull, Oggin was on his way in. He knew that people in here were builders with delicious sandwich. If they didn't offer him any he knew where to find them.

"Oggin," said Robert. "You shouldn't be here."

"That's what you think," said Oggin's smile, when he saw hundreds of builders sitting in chairs waiting to feed him. And, after all, this had been his field until a few months ago, and there might still be mice.

At the other end of the room everybody

was watching something else. The dog pushed the basin again, and gave a little yelp. It knew about milky tea. Dogs do, thought Robert. That's all.

The children were reaching out hands to pat the dog, but their arms were not long enough, or something. Robert put Oggin on his knee and told him to behave, or he would have extra spelling and more yucky dinners with the infant class. Of course, Oggin liked yucky dinners. "Or wiping the tables down," said Robert.

Mrs Arkwright knew what to do about the dog, without fussing over the rules. She bent down and poured her tea into the basin.

"What's going on?" said the end of Oggin's tail, twitching a bit. "I'm going to do something about it," said his elbows, digging into Robert's knee like fangs.

Mrs Arkwright had done the right thing, under the lamplight. The dog put its muzzle into the basin and drank the tea. Then it lifted it head, sat down, and licked its lips.

"And then what?" said Dad. "Remember what she used to say, Oz?"

One or two other people said they remembered too.

"Say it then," said Oz.

"I left the old school forty years ago," said Dad. "Coco, that was its name" (and the dog waved its tail once) "used to come down, and get its tea. And then Mrs Furlong would say . . . but it sounds daft to say it now . . . even if some people still know."

"Go on," said Oz. "You heard it often enough, Bernard."

"She used to say . . . should I say it now?"

"Go on," said Mum.

"It would be quite proper," said Mr Arkwright. Mum nodding away to agree.

"She used to tell him where to go, and who to,'" said Dad. "And off he would go. Now, Coco," he went on, and the dog looked at him, but as if he wasn't quite the right person. "Go home to Daddy. That's it, Go home to Daddy."

The dog stood up. He had had his orders. He sniffed at the basin once more, just in case, realised it was empty and wouldn't be filled, and wagged his tail gently, regretfully.

Under the lamplight his tail began not to be quite so distinct, as if the light was beginning to go through it. He was leaving, going home to Daddy.

"It's goodbye," said Oz, gently. "You came

back Coco, or you never left the last time."

"To wherever," said Dad, "from wherever."

Mum sniffed. She understood about coming back to do some duty or other, and then leaving for ever. "And we didn't know who he was," she said. "We just wanted him out of the way."

At the back of the room Oggin put on his winter tyres with spikes and accelerated off Robert's knee, leaving deep ruts in his thigh. He meant, "This is still my field, and I am doing something about intruders; my duty towards Dog."

He was on the floor now, and stalking his enemy, finding his way through a forest of legs and among the roots of feet. He was speaking out loud now, using words not allowed in school. He was also getting bigger, fluffed up

106

like a hairy pumpkin.

The dog began to turn towards the entrance hall door, ready to leave by walking. But he was not going to leave by walking. As it crossed the floor its feet, touching the floor in the usual way to begin with, began not to touch it, to fade away, like his tail, and not be there.

Its tail, and its feet, could no longer be seen.

But there was still enough dog for Oggin to understand. Cats do not mind about dogs floating. They think it is natural. They go for the bit they can see, ribs, and belly, and face, slap, slap across the face. They understand eyes and the tenderness of noses.

Oggin knew all that. He understood about ears too, or why would he make terrifying noises, bigger than himself?

Oggin going in to the attack, sudden, in full battle array, not to be stopped, and in any case there first. Not bothering to walk, but flying, propulsion happening.

The dog walked those few feet towards the hall door, and as it approached the rest of it disappeared too, the head becoming fainter and fainter, the body turning grey and melting from sight.

Oggin was upon him before he left. Oggin had burst into a multitude of claws and fangs whirling round the big orange centre. Like a tiger-fur Swiss Army Knife, Robert thought, with multiple blades, scissors, corkscrews, spikes, screwdrivers, all active, ready to go and going, with menace switched on loud.

And then switched off, Oggin silent, Oggin

on the floor, Oggin sitting there, large and spread-eagled, wondering what he had been doing, hoping no one else had seen his hallucination, and that this was some other Oggin, not the one we know, not his fault at all.

Because the dog had completed his vanishing before getting to the door. By the time Oggin got to him with all missiles armed and in the air, the dog had completely gone. It had not gone anywhere, so it could not be followed. It had simply stopped existing at all.

Oggin sat down. He scratched his left ear. He got up and looked at the dog's basin. It was empty.

The children all said "Aah," thinking it had been a wonderful trick. People from the Education Department thought they ought to be going, and assumed it was a joke, or that there was no discipline in this school, and something would be done about it. The Governors knew that something real but unexplained had happened, and that it had been right, and should have happened. So they had second cups of tea, because the matter was over. The dog had had its day, because every dog does have his day.

"I think," said Mr Arkwright, "that the spirit of the old school, and quite a lot of forgotten items, have been brought here by that dog, to remind us of older times and often wiser heads. This new building has somehow been brought up to date by the visits of something from an older time. And I shall remember this first day of meeting everybody and of being met by the old school all the time I am here."

"It's a queer do," said Dad. "But it fits right in, eh, Oz?"

"Old times, new times," said Oz. "But that's what it was then."

So they had conversations with others who remembered the same thing happening all those years ago. And how Coco had been better liked than the pupils ("Scholars," said Dad) had been.

"But a lot to be said for the old days," said Mr Arkwright. "And nothing changes. Even the spelling is the same." He was showing people the bundle of knotted threads, and they were picking out the words, and sometimes wondering whether they had written them.

Others were searching the old register and finding their parents and grandparents.

Robert went back to the end of the table.

The stray sausage roll was still looking for a home. There was just the danger of Oggin getting there first, leaping out from under the table.

But it was Joanne's head coming from under the hanging folds of the tablecloth, and it was Joanne's hand reaching for the sausage roll. Mum who saw it all, and fetched Robert another from another plate, with a recommending smile.

Oggin had made a friend. Under the table he and Joanne shared the sausage roll, her on the floor, him on a chair, two redheads curled up together, eating with their fingers. She's lucky it's not a green cat, thought Robert. Green hair, just suit her, yeah.

Somewhere outside, in the present or in the past, the dog called Coco went the last time home to Daddy.

Mum took the basin home and washed it. It lives in a cupboard in the infant room, and is put beside anyone who feels ghostly in the middle. It's been in patient training a hundred years.

The feeling usually vanishes. Or the sickly infant goes home to Mummy.